KT-564-739

THE STINKY SPROUTS

Rosie Greening ▪ Stuart Lynch

make
believe
ideas

In a faraway kitchen,
there lived lots of **FOOD:**

some **silly,** some **clever**
and some **rather rude!**

The **CARROTS** were **SPORTY**,
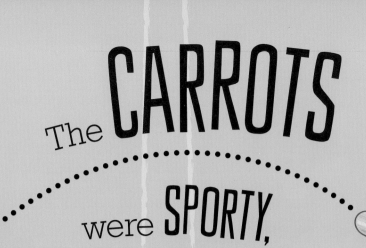
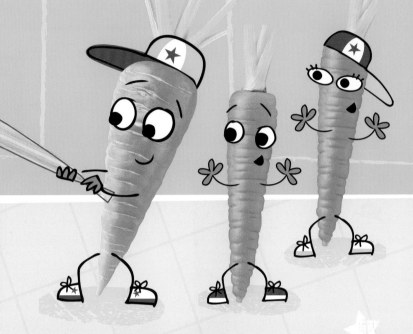

the **BEANS** enjoyed **books**,

the **TURNIPS** told **JOKES**,

and the **LEEKS** loved their **looks!**

Although they were different, they **hung** out EACH DAY.

But one GROUP was never invited to PLAY . . .

This squad was the **SPROUTS,**
and their **smell** was so **STRONG**
that **no one** could stand
to be **near** them for long.

So when they rolled by, all the others would shout:

"Take a breath, **hold your nose** – I can SMELL STINKY SPROUTS."

But while the **bad smell** made the other **veg** FLEE,

underneath the **SPROUTS' PONG,** they were **SWEET** as can be.

"If we could smell nice," Mrs Sprout said one day,

"the others might like us, and not **RUN AWAY."**

So all of the **SPROUTS** got together to think.
But **NO ONE** knew how
to get rid of the
stink!

At last, **Sadie SPROUT** said,

"Come on, **follow** me!"

Then jumped in some **CRANBERRY** sauce

with a "**WHEEEEE!**"

Her **family** thought
Sadie **SPROUT** had gone **mad.**

CLIMBED

But when she **CLIMBED** out, she no **longer** smelled **BAD!**

The **sweet,** STICKY sauce

had disguised **Sadie's** SMELL,

and **made** her as PINK
as a PETAL as well.

And so, **one** by **one,**
all the **SPROUTS** got in line,

to **SWIM** in the sauce
and start **smelling divine.**

Mr **SPROUT** said, **"IT'S PERFECT,"**
and started to **grin.**

"Now maybe the **others**
will let us **join in."**

The **sweet-smelling** SPROUTS

found the cool **CARROT CREW**

and asked them **politely,**

"Can we play with you?"

"**Of course,**" they replied.

"We've not seen you before, but since you smell **SWEET**, you can **join us, for sure.**"

"They don't know it's us!" said the SPROUTS in **surprise.**

"This pink, sticky **sauce** is the **PERFECT** disguise."

So they **joked** with the **TURNIPS** . . . .

and **PLAYED** with the **PEAS.**

With their **stunning** new scent, making friends was a **BREEZE!**

Then the cool **CARROT** crew **dared** the SPROUTS to a **race**.

The **SPROUTS** thought, **"We've made it,"** and rushed into place.

But once they were rolling, a **tragedy** struck: their **cranberry sauce** started coming **UNSTUCK!**

And as the **SAUCE** trickled **and DRIPPED** to the floor,

the **SPROUTS** became

STINKY

and **green** as before!

The other **VEG** gasped, recognising the **PONG.**

A **PARSNIP** cried out, **"You were SPROUTS all along!"**

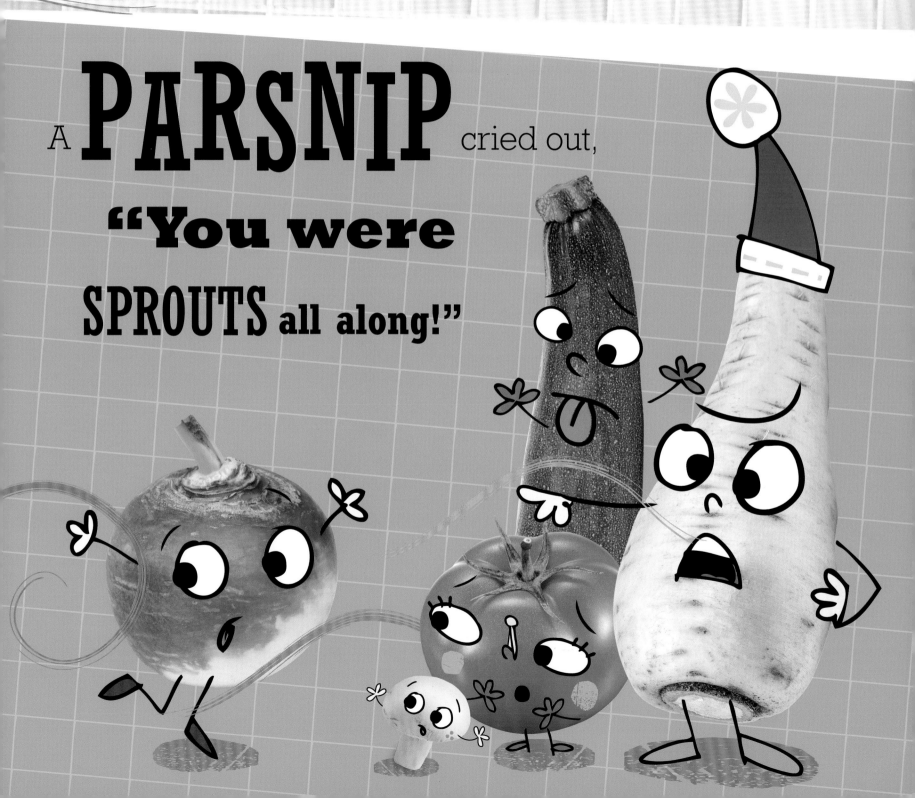

The **SPROUTS** turned to leave,

but their **friends** shouted, **"NO!**

Today was such fun,

WE DON'T WANT YOU TO GO."

They said,

"We thought **NOTHING** smelled worse than a **SPROUT**.

But we were the **stinkers** for **leaving** you out!"

The others had **learnt**
that their **actions** were **WRONG** —
they shouldn't have **judged**
all the **SPROUTS** by their **PONG.**

So from that day onwards, **the groups got on well.**

And they loved the
SPROUTS dearly,
in spite of their SMELL!